P9-ELU-791

Here's what kids and grown-ups have to say about the Magic Tree House® books:

"Oh, man . . . the Magic Tree House series
is really exciting!"
—Christina

"I like the Magic Tree House series. I stay up
all night reading them. Even on school nights!"
—Peter

"Jack and Annie have opened a door to a world
of literacy that I know will continue throughout
the lives of my students."
—Deborah H.

"As a librarian, I have seen many happy young
readers coming into the library to check out
the next Magic Tree House book in the series."
Lynne H.

Magic Tree House®

For a list of Magic Tree House® Merlin Missions and other Magic Tree House® titles, visit MagicTreeHouse.com.

MAGIC TREE HOUSE®

#18 BUFFALO BEFORE BREAKFAST

BY MARY POPE OSBORNE
ILLUSTRATED BY SAL MURDOCCA

A STEPPING STONE BOOK™

Random House 🏠 New York

For Natalie,
kind and funny grandmother
of Andrew and Peter

Text copyright © 1999 by Mary Pope Osborne
Cover art and interior illustrations copyright © 1999 by Sal Murdocca

All rights reserved. Published in the United States by Random House Children's Books, a division of Penguin Random House LLC, New York.

Random House and the colophon are registered trademarks and A Stepping Stone Book and the colophon are trademarks of Penguin Random House LLC. Magic Tree House is a registered trademark of Mary Pope Osborne; used under license.

Visit us on the Web!
randomhousekids.com
MagicTreeHouse.com

Educators and librarians, for a variety of teaching tools, visit us at
RHTeachersLibrarians.com

Library of Congress Cataloging-in-Publication Data
Osborne, Mary Pope.
Buffalo before breakfast / by Mary Pope Osborne ; illustrated by Sal Murdocca.
p. cm. — (Magic tree house ; #18) "A stepping stone book."
Summary: The magic tree house takes Jack and his sister Annie to the Great Plains, where they learn about the life of the Lakota Indians.
ISBN 978-0-679-89064-5 (pbk.) — ISBN 978-0-679-99064-2 (lib. bdg.) — ISBN 978-0-375-89475-6 (ebook)
[1. Time travel—Fiction. 2. Magic—Fiction. 3. Tree houses—Fiction. 4. Dakota Indians—Fiction. 5. Indians of North America—Great Plains—Fiction.] I. Murdocca, Sal, ill. II. Title. III. Series: Osborne, Mary Pope. Magic tree house series ; 18.
PZ7.O81167Bu 1999 [Fic]—dc21 98-37089

Printed in the United States of America 52 51 50 49 48 47

This book has been officially leveled by using the F&P Text Level Gradient™ Leveling System.

Contents

Prologue

One summer day in Frog Creek, Pennsylvania, a mysterious tree house appeared in the woods.

Eight-year-old Jack and his seven-year-old sister, Annie, climbed into the tree house. They found it was filled with books.

Jack and Annie soon discovered that the tree house was magic. It could take them to the places in the books. All they had to do was point to a picture and wish to go there.

Along the way, Jack and Annie discovered that the tree house belongs to Morgan le Fay. Morgan is a magical librarian from the time of King Arthur. She travels through time and space, gathering books.

In Magic Tree House Books #5–8, Jack and Annie helped free Morgan from a spell. In books #9–12, they solved four ancient riddles and became Master Librarians.

In Magic Tree House Books #13–16, Jack and Annie had to save four ancient stories from being lost forever.

In Magic Tree House Books #17–20, Jack and Annie must be given four special gifts to help free a mysterious dog from a magic spell. They have already received one gift on a trip to the *Titanic*. And now they are about to set out in search of the second gift. . . .

1

Teddy's Back!

Arf! Arf! Arf!

Jack finished tying his sneakers. Then he looked out his bedroom window.

A small dog stood in the early sunlight. He had floppy ears and scruffy brown fur.

"Teddy!" said Jack.

Just then, Annie ran into Jack's room.

"Teddy's back!" she said. "It's time."

It was time for their second mission to help free the little dog from a spell.

Jack threw his notebook and pencil into his backpack. Then he followed Annie downstairs and past the kitchen.

"Where are you two going?" their mom called.

"Outside," said Jack.

"Breakfast will be ready soon," she said. "And Grandmother will be here any minute."

"We'll be right back," said Jack. He loved his grandmother's visits. She was kind and funny. And she always taught them new things.

Jack and Annie slipped out the front door. Teddy was waiting for them.

Arf! Arf! he barked.

"Hey, where did you go last week?" Jack asked.

The small dog wagged his tail joyfully.

Then he ran up the sidewalk.

"Wait for us!" Annie shouted.

She and Jack followed Teddy up the street and into the Frog Creek woods.

They ran between the trees. Wind rattled the leaves. Birds swooped from branch to branch.

Teddy stopped at a rope ladder that hung from the tallest oak tree in the woods. At the top of the ladder was the magic tree house.

Jack and Annie stared up at it.

"No sign of Morgan," said Annie.

"Let's go up," said Jack.

Annie picked up Teddy. She carried him carefully up the ladder. Jack climbed after her.

Inside the tree house, Teddy sniffed a silver pocket watch on the floor. Beside it was

the note that Morgan had written to Jack and
Annie.

Annie picked up the note and read it aloud:

*This little dog is under a spell and needs
your help. To free him, you must be given
four special things:*

A gift from a ship lost at sea,
A gift from the prairie blue,
A gift from a forest far away,
A gift from a kangaroo.
Be brave. Be wise. Be careful.

"We've got the first special thing," said
Annie, "the gift from a ship lost at sea."

"Yeah," said Jack. He picked up the silver
pocket watch.

The time on the watch was 2:20—the time
the *Titanic* had sunk.

7

Jack and Annie stared at the watch.

Arf! Arf!

Teddy's barking brought Jack back from his memories.

"Okay," Jack said. He sighed and pushed his glasses into place. "Now it's time for the gift from the prairie blue."

"What's that mean?" said Annie.

"I'm not sure," said Jack. He looked around the tree house. "But I bet that book will take us there."

He picked up a book in the corner. The cover was a picture of a wide prairie. The title was *The Great Plains*.

"Ready?" Jack said.

Teddy yipped and wagged his tail.

"Let's go," said Annie. "The sooner we free Teddy, the better."

Jack pointed at the cover.

"I wish we could go there," he said.

The wind started to blow.

The tree house started to spin.

It spun faster and faster.

Then everything was still.

Absolutely still.

2

Ocean of Grass

Early sunlight slanted into the tree house. The cool breeze smelled of wild grass.

"Oh, man," said Jack. "These are neat clothes."

Their jeans and T-shirts had magically changed. Jack had on a buckskin shirt and pants. Annie wore a fringed buckskin dress.

They both wore soft leather boots and coonskin caps. Jack's backpack was now a leather bag.

"I feel like a mountain man," he said.

"All you're missing is a mountain," said Annie. She pointed out the window.

Jack and Teddy looked out.

The tree house sat in a lone tree in a vast golden prairie. The sun was rising in the distance.

Wind whispered through the tall yellow grass. *Shh—shh—shh*, it said.

"We need a gift from the prairie blue," said Jack.

"I bet that means the sky," said Annie, looking up.

"Yep," said Jack. The sky was growing bluer as they watched. "But how are we supposed to get it?"

"Just like last time," said Annie. "We have to wait till someone gives it to us."

"I don't see any sign of people out there," said Jack.

He opened their book and read aloud.

> The Great Plains are in the middle
> of the United States. Before the 20th
> century, this vast prairie covered
> nearly a fifth of America's land. Some
> called it "an ocean of grass."

Jack pulled out his notebook.

"Come on," said Annie.

She picked up Teddy and carried him down the ladder.

Jack quickly wrote:

Great Plains — lots of land

"Wow, this *is* like an ocean of grass," Annie called from below.

Jack slipped the Great Plains book and his notebook into his leather bag and climbed down.

When he stepped onto the ground, the grass came all the way up to his chest. It tickled his nose.

"*Ah-ah-CHOO!*" he sneezed.

"Let's go swimming in the grass ocean," said Annie.

She started off with Teddy under her arm.

The wind blew gently as Jack hurried after her. All he could see was rolling waves of grass.

They walked and walked and walked. Finally, they stopped to rest.

"We could walk for months and never see anything but grass," said Jack.

Arf! Arf!

"Teddy says there's something great up ahead," said Annie.

"You can't tell what he's saying," said Jack. "He's just barking."

"I *can* tell," said Annie. "Trust me."

"We can't walk all day," said Jack.

"Come on," said Annie. "Just a little farther." She started walking again.

"Oh, brother," said Jack.

But he kept going through the tall, rippling grass. They went down a small slope, then up a small rise. At the top of the rise, Jack froze.

"Wow, that *is* great," he whispered.

"Told you," said Annie.

3

Black Hawk

Jack stared at a circle of tepees ahead. Busy people in buckskins moved about the circle. Horses and ponies grazed nearby.

Jack took out their research book and found a picture of the tepees.

He read:

> In the early 1800s, many different
> Native American tribes lived on the
> Great Plains. The Lakota were the

largest tribe. They lived mostly in the areas we now call North Dakota, South Dakota, and Minnesota.

Jack pulled out his notebook and wrote:

early 1800s—Lakota were largest tribe of Great Plains

Behind Jack and Annie, a horse neighed. They turned. A horse and rider were heading toward the tepee camp.

The sun was very bright behind the
rider. Jack could only see the outline of
a body with a bow and a quiver of arrows on
his back.

Jack quickly flipped through the book. He found a picture of a man on horseback carrying a bow and arrows. Below the picture it said LAKOTA WARRIOR.

Jack read:

> Everything changed for the Native Americans of the Great Plains after white settlers arrived in the mid-1800s. Fighting broke out between Lakota warriors and white soldiers. By the end of the 1800s, the Lakota were defeated. They lost both their land and their old way of life.

Jack looked back at the rider. The warrior was coming closer.

"Get down," he whispered.

"Why?" said Annie.

"This might be a time when the Indians

are fighting with the settlers," said Jack.

The grass rustled as the warrior passed by them. His horse neighed again.

Arf! Arf!

"Shh!" whispered Jack.

But it was too late. The warrior had heard Teddy's barking. He galloped toward them, grabbing his bow.

"Wait!" shouted Jack. He jumped up from the grass. "We come in peace!"

The rider halted.

Now Jack saw that he was only a boy on a pony. He couldn't have been more than ten or eleven.

"Hey, you're just a kid," Annie said, smiling.

The boy didn't smile back. But he did lower his bow while he stared at Annie.

"What's your name?" she asked.

"Black Hawk," he said.

"Cool name," said Annie. "We're Jack and Annie. We're just visiting. We live in Frog Creek, Pennsylvania."

Black Hawk nodded. Then he turned his pony around and started toward the Lakota camp.

"Hey, can we come with you?" called Annie.

Black Hawk looked back.

"Yes," he said. "Meet my people."

"You mean your parents?" asked Annie.

"No, they died long ago," said Black Hawk. "I live with my grandmother."

"Oh, I'd like to meet your grandmother," said Annie. "I'm going to see my grandmother today, too."

Black Hawk nudged his pony forward again. Annie followed with Teddy.

Jack didn't move.

What if the Lakota are at war with the white settlers? he worried. *What if they think we're enemies?*

"Annie!" Jack called softly. "We don't know if it's safe or not!"

But Annie just waved for him to come on.

Jack sighed. He opened the research book and quickly flipped through the pages. He wanted information about how to act with the Lakota.

On one page, he read:

> Good manners to the Lakota mean speaking as few words as possible and sharing gifts when visiting.

On another page, he read:

**The Lakota admire those who do not
show fear.**

Jack's favorite piece of information was:

Holding up two fingers means "friend."

Jack put the book away. He ran to catch
up with Annie.

Annie was telling Black Hawk all about
their grandmother. The boy listened silently.

"Annie," Jack whispered. "I just read that
it's good manners to be quiet. And we should
give gifts and not show fear. Also, holding up
two fingers means 'friend.'"

Annie nodded.

"Got that?" said Jack.

"Sure," she said. "No talking, no fear, no problem."

Jack looked up. He caught his breath.

Ahead of them, the people at the campsite had stopped what they were doing. All eyes were turned to Jack and Annie.

Jack quickly held up two fingers. Annie did the same.

4

Good Manners

Black Hawk led Jack and Annie toward the tepees. Everyone kept watching them.

Jack couldn't tell what anyone was thinking. No one looked angry. But no one looked happy, either.

Jack wondered how to appear brave.

He glanced at Annie. She walked tall and straight. Her chin was up. Her face was calm.

Jack straightened his shoulders. He lifted his chin, and he felt braver.

Black Hawk stopped and slid off his pony. The pony headed for the grazing pasture.

Then Black Hawk led them to a tepee. It was covered with buffalo designs.

"Grandmother is inside," Black Hawk said to Jack and Annie.

Inside, the tepee looked like a small round room. A fire burned in the center. Smoke rose through a hole at the top.

An old woman sat on animal skins. She was sewing beads onto a moccasin.

She looked up at Jack and Annie.

"Grandmother," said Black Hawk. "This is Jack and Annie from Frog Creek, Pennsylvania."

Jack and Annie both held up two fingers for "friend."

Grandmother raised two fingers also.

Then Jack took off his coonskin cap. He gave it to Grandmother.

She put the cap on her head, then laughed. Jack and Annie laughed, too.

Grandmother's laughter and kind face reminded Jack of his own grandmother.

"You wish to learn our ways," she said.

Jack and Annie nodded. Jack could tell she was wise.

Grandmother stood and left the tepee. They followed her.

Outside, everyone was busy again. They all seemed to know that Jack and Annie weren't enemies.

Jack looked around the camp.

Men and boys carved bows. Women and girls pounded meat and sewed clothes. One girl was adding claws to a buckskin shirt.

"The bear claws will give her the strength of the bear," said Grandmother. "She will sew on hawk feathers, elk teeth, and porcupine quills, too. All will give her the power of the animals."

Jack pulled out his notebook and wrote:

Sew bear claws to shirt

"I have strong animal power when I go on a buffalo hunt," Black Hawk said proudly.

"What do you mean?" asked Jack.

"I will show you," said Black Hawk. "Wait."

Black Hawk went back inside the tepee.

Annie turned to Grandmother.

"Why does he hunt the buffalo?" she asked.

"The buffalo gives our people many gifts," said the old woman. "Food from his body. Tepees from his skin, tools from his bones."

Jack started making a list.

"Cups from his horns," Grandmother went on. "Ropes from his hair. Even winter sleds from his ribs."

Jack finished his list.

<u>buffalo</u>
skin—tepee
bones—tools
horns—cups
hair—ropes
ribs—sleds

"That reminds me of the seal hunter in the

29

Arctic," said Annie. "He used all the gifts from the seal's body. He didn't waste a thing."

Just then, Teddy began growling and barking.

Jack and Annie turned around. They both gasped.

Coming out of Grandmother's tepee was a huge wolf!

5

Sunlight and Midnight

The wolf had yellow eyes and sharp teeth.

Teddy snarled and barked. Annie rushed forward to grab the little dog.

Suddenly the wolf stood up on its hind legs!

"Yikes!" said Annie.

She leaped back.

Then she and Jack started to laugh.

The fierce wolf was Black Hawk wearing a wolf's hide! His head came out through a slit near the wolf's neck. He gave Jack and Annie a little smile.

"That's a great wolf suit," said Annie.

"Why do you wear that?" asked Jack.

"The wolf is the most powerful hunter of the buffalo," said Black Hawk. "When I wear his skin, I feel his strength."

"Wow," said Annie.

Black Hawk looked at his grandmother.

"May I show them the buffalo now?" he said.

"Only *show*," said Grandmother. "Do not hunt. We have enough meat today."

She looked back at Jack and Annie.

"Lakota never take more buffalo than we need," she said.

"That's good," said Annie.

Black Hawk handed his wolf skin to

Grandmother. Then he ran to the grazing ponies.

He climbed on his. Then he herded two ponies, one black and one yellow, over to Jack and Annie.

"Hi, Midnight. Hi, Sunlight," said Annie, naming the ponies. She patted their noses.

"Annie," whispered Jack. "How are we going to ride without saddles or reins?"

"Just hold on to their manes," she said, "and grip with your legs. Watch."

Annie threw her arms around Midnight's neck. She slung her leg over the pony's back and pulled herself up.

"I'll carry Teddy in the bag," Annie said.

Jack picked up Teddy and slipped him inside the leather bag. He handed it to Annie, who hung it over her shoulder. Teddy's head peeked out of the bag.

Arf! he barked.

"Giddy-up, Midnight!" said Annie. The pony started to walk away.

"Wait—" said Jack.

He turned to Black Hawk. He had just a few questions.

Black Hawk let out a wild whoop and took off, too.

Jack took a deep breath. He threw his arms around Sunlight's neck. Then he slung his leg over the pony's back.

The pony started to move!

"Wait—wait!" said Jack. He hopped on one foot, trying to keep up.

The pony stopped.

Slowly, Jack pulled himself onto Sunlight's back. He gripped the pony's mane. Then he carefully reached up and pushed his glasses into place.

He looked over his shoulder. Grandmother was watching.

She nodded at him.

Lakota people admire those who do not show fear, Jack remembered.

He liked Grandmother. He wanted her to admire him. He let out a wild whoop, and Sunlight took off like the wind.

The whoop made Jack feel braver.

He held tightly to Sunlight's mane. They caught up with Black Hawk and Annie, and together they all rode through the tall grass.

Shadows of clouds swept over the plains. They looked like giant dark birds spreading their wings.

Black Hawk's pony stopped at the top of a

grassy slope. Sunlight and Midnight halted right behind him.

Jack couldn't believe his eyes.

Before them were thousands and thousands of grazing buffalo.

6

Stampede!

"Wow," whispered Jack and Annie together.

Black Hawk looked silently at the grazing buffalo.

"Hand me the research book," said Jack.

Annie lifted Teddy out of the bag. Then she slid the book out and gave it to Jack.

He found a picture of a buffalo herd. He read to himself.

> The true name of the buffalo is "bison."
> At the beginning of the 1800s, there

were 40 million bison on the Great
Plains. One hundred years later, there
were less than 300. Almost all had been
killed by white hunters and soldiers.

Jack looked back at the vast herd. As far
as he could see, there was nothing but buffalo.

Now Jack knew for certain they'd come to the time *before* the white settlers and soldiers had arrived, *before* the end of the great buffalo herds.

"I have been on many hunts," Black Hawk said, his eyes still on the buffalo.

"Were you scared?" said Jack.

Black Hawk shook his head.

"You're really brave," said Annie.

Black Hawk smiled proudly.

"I will show you how a brave hunter moves," he said.

He slid off his pony.

"Wait, your grandmother said not to hunt," said Annie. "Plus, you don't have your wolf suit."

"I am not afraid," said Black Hawk.

"I don't think you should go down there,"

said Jack. "There's no grownups around."

But Black Hawk wasn't listening.

He began creeping on all fours toward the buffalo.

"I have a feeling something bad is going to happen," said Annie.

Jack had the same feeling. He looked back at the book.

> A bison can weigh two thousand pounds and stand six feet high. If one becomes alarmed by a hunter, he might start running and set off a terrifying stampede.

Jack looked back at Black Hawk. He was creeping closer and closer to the herd.

Jack's heart pounded. He wanted to shout, *Come back!* But he didn't want to scare any of the huge, fierce-looking animals.

Keeping his eyes on Black Hawk, Jack handed the plains book to Annie. She slid it back into the bag beside Teddy.

Black Hawk stopped just as he was passing the nearest buffalo. His eyes squeezed shut. His nose wrinkled up. His mouth opened.

"What's he doing?" asked Jack.

"*Ah-ah-CHOO!*" Black Hawk sneezed.

"Uh-oh," said Annie.

The huge buffalo jerked its head up. It made a low, moaning sound. Then it pointed its horns and charged!

"Watch out!" cried Jack.

Black Hawk threw himself out of the way of the charging buffalo.

A ripple went through the herd as other shaggy animals looked up.

Suddenly, Teddy jumped out of Annie's arms. He landed in the tall grass and ran toward the buffalo.

"Teddy!" shouted Annie.

The dog tore down the hill. He bounded along the edge of the herd, barking furiously.

"Teddy, come back!" cried Annie.

She slid off her pony and ran after Teddy.

Jack tried to see Black Hawk.

The boy was still dodging the running buffalo. He looked tired.

Jack took a deep breath.

"Go to Black Hawk!" he said, nudging Sunlight with his knees.

The golden pony charged down the slope. He ran between the buffalo.

"Black Hawk!" Jack shouted.

Black Hawk started running toward Sunlight. The buffalo swerved behind him.

Sunlight slowed as Black Hawk got near. The boy threw himself over the golden pony's back. He held on to Jack as Sunlight veered away from the buffalo and ran back up the slope.

"Where's Annie?" Jack cried as they reached the top.

"There!" said Black Hawk, pointing.

Annie was surrounded by buffalo—*calm* buffalo. She was patting them and talking to them. The buffalo near her had stopped running, too.

The ones beyond those started to calm down . . . then others . . . until all the buffalo had stopped running. They began grazing again as if nothing had happened.

7

White Buffalo Woman

"She has good medicine," said Black Hawk.

"Annie doesn't have any medicine," Jack said. "She just has a way with animals."

Black Hawk was silent. He climbed back on his waiting pony. Then he rode down toward Annie.

Jack followed. Annie's pony trailed behind.

Annie turned to Jack and Black Hawk as they rode up to her. On her face was a look of amazement.

"You wouldn't believe what happened!" she said.

"You stopped the stampede," said Black Hawk.

"But it wasn't just me," said Annie.

"What do you mean?" asked Jack.

"I was trying to find Teddy," said Annie, "and I got in the way of the buffalo. I couldn't escape. So I held up my hands and shouted, '*Stop!*' Then, out of nowhere, a beautiful lady in a white leather dress came to help me."

"You saw a lady in white?" asked Black Hawk. His eyes had grown wide.

"Yes!" said Annie. "She held up *her* hands, and the buffalo stopped running. Then she disappeared."

"Where's Teddy?" said Jack.

Annie gasped.

"I don't know! I forgot about him!" she said. "Teddy! Teddy!"

Arf! Arf!

The little dog came bounding out of the grass toward them.

Annie scooped him up. Teddy licked her face all over.

"Where did you go?" Annie asked him. "Did you see the beautiful lady, too?"

"That lady does not live on this earth," Black Hawk said softly.

"What do you mean?" said Annie.

"You saw the spirit of White Buffalo Woman," he said.

"What do you mean, *spirit?*" said Jack. "You mean like a ghost?"

Black Hawk turned his pony around.

"Let us go back," he said. "We must tell Grandmother."

Annie put Teddy in Jack's bag. Then she climbed on her pony, and they took off.

Behind them, the buffalo grazed peacefully on the plains.

8

Sacred Circle

The sun was going down as the three ponies galloped for home. The deep blue sky was streaked with golden red light.

Back at the Lakota camp, the circle of tepees glowed in the setting sun. People were gathered around a large fire.

Black Hawk led Jack and Annie to the camp. They got off their ponies and went over to the fire.

Grandmother rose to greet them.

"You have been gone a long time," she said.

Black Hawk looked her bravely in the eye.

"Grandmother, I tried to hunt the buffalo alone," he said. "One charged at me, but Jack saved my life. Then Annie and White Buffalo Woman stopped all the other buffalo from a stampede."

"Let this be a lesson to you," Grandmother said sternly. "Your pride led you to show off. Showing off made you behave foolishly. Your foolishness frightened a buffalo. He frightened others. One thing always leads to another. Everything is related."

"I am sorry," said Black Hawk. He hung his head. "I have learned."

Jack felt sorry for Black Hawk.

"I make mistakes sometimes, too," he said softly.

"Me too," said Annie.

Grandmother looked at Jack and Annie.

"Buffalo Girl and Rides-Like-Wind showed great courage today," she said.

Jack smiled. He loved his new Lakota name: *Rides-Like-Wind*.

"We welcome you to our family," said Grandmother.

The evening shadows spread over the camp. Someone began beating a drum. It sounded like a heartbeat.

"Come, sit with us in our circle," said Grandmother.

They sat with her near the warm fire. A cool breeze blew sparks into the gray twilight.

An old man held a long pipe up to the sky.
He pointed it to the east, the south, the west,
and the north.

Then he passed the pipe to the next man

in the circle. The man put the pipe to his lips
and blew smoke into the golden firelight.
Then he passed it on.

"The smoke from the sacred pipe joins all

things to the Great Spirit," Grandmother said to Jack and Annie.

"The Great Spirit?" asked Annie.

"The Great Spirit is the source of all things in the sacred circle of life," said Grandmother. "It is the source of all spirits."

"What spirits?" asked Jack.

"There are many," said Grandmother. "Wind spirits, tree spirits, bird spirits. Sometimes they can be seen. Sometimes not."

"What about the White Buffalo Woman?" said Jack. "Who is she?"

"She is a messenger of the Great Spirit," said Grandmother. "He sent her when the people were starving. She brought the sacred pipe so that our prayers could rise to the Great Spirit. He answers by sending us the buffalo."

"Why do you think White Buffalo Woman came to me?" asked Annie.

"Sometimes courage can summon help from the beyond," Grandmother said.

She pulled a brown-and-white feather from a small buckskin bag.

She put the feather on the ground in front of Jack and Annie.

"This is a gift for you," she said. "An eagle's feather for your courage."

Arf! Arf! Teddy wagged his tail.

Jack and Annie smiled at each other. The eagle's feather was their "gift from the prairie blue."

Their mission was complete.

The chanting and drumbeats grew louder and louder. Then they stopped.

The old man held the pipe up to the sky.

"All things are related," he said.

The pipe-smoking ceremony was over.

The sky was dark and filled with stars.

One by one, people rose from the circle and went to their tepees.

Jack put the eagle's feather in his bag and yawned.

"We better go home now," he said.

"You must rest first," said Grandmother. "You can leave in the dawn."

"Good plan," said Annie. She was yawning, too.

They went with Grandmother and Black Hawk to their tepee.

Grandmother pointed to two buffalo robes that lay to one side of the still-burning fire. Jack and Annie stretched out on them. Teddy snuggled between them.

Grandmother and Black Hawk lay on robes across from them.

Jack watched as the bluish white smoke rose from the fire. It went up through the tepee hole and into the endless starry sky.

Jack listened to the wind blowing through the grass: *Shh—shh—shh.*

It's the voice of the Great Plains, he thought. Then he drifted off to sleep.

9

Lakota School

Jack felt Teddy licking his cheek.

He opened his eyes. Gray light came through the smoke hole.

The fire was out. The tepee was empty.

Jack jumped up. He grabbed his bag and hurried outside with Teddy.

In the cool light before dawn, everyone was taking down their tepees. They were loading them onto wooden platforms strapped to two poles. The poles were pulled by horses.

Grandmother and Black Hawk piled tools and clothes onto their platform.

Annie stuffed buffalo meat into a rawhide bag.

"What's happening?" Jack asked.

"It is time to follow the buffalo," said Grandmother. "We will camp somewhere else for a few weeks."

Jack pulled out his notebook. He still had many questions. But he tried to choose just a few.

"Can you camp anywhere?" he asked. "Even when you don't own the land?"

Black Hawk laughed.

"People cannot own land," he said. "The land belongs to the Great Spirit."

Jack wrote in his notebook:

land owned by Great Spirit, not people

"What about school?" said Jack. "Don't you have to go to school?"

"What is school?" Black Hawk said.

"It's a place where kids go to learn things," Jack explained.

Black Hawk laughed again.

"There is not only one place to learn," he said. "In camp we learn to make clothes, tools, and tepees. On the plains we learn to ride and hunt. We look at the sky and learn courage from the eagle."

Jack wrote:

Lakota school is everywhere

Grandmother turned to Jack and Annie.

"Will you walk with us toward the sunset?" she asked.

Jack shook his head.

"We have to go the other way," he said, "toward the sunrise."

"Thank you for the eagle's feather," said Annie.

"Let your thoughts rise as high as that feather," said Grandmother. "It is good medicine."

"What does that mean?" Jack asked. *"Good medicine?"*

"Good medicine connects you to the world of the spirits," she said.

Jack nodded. But he still didn't really understand.

"Good-bye, Buffalo Girl and Rides-Like-Wind," said Grandmother. "We wish you a safe journey."

Jack and Annie waved. Then they started walking back the way they'd come.

Teddy ran ahead of them.

At the top of the rise, they looked back.

Grandmother, Black Hawk, and the rest of the tribe were watching.

Jack and Annie both held up two fingers for "friend." Then they took off down the slope.

They ran across the prairie . . . through the tall, whispering grass . . . all the way back to the tree house.

Annie put Teddy in the leather bag. She and Jack climbed up the rope ladder.

They looked out the window one last time. The ocean of grass was golden in the early sunlight.

By now, the Lakota are walking west, Jack thought.

"Soon everything will change," he said sadly. "The buffalo will vanish. The old way of life for the Lakota will vanish, too."

"But the Great Spirit won't ever vanish," said Annie. "It will *always* take care of Black Hawk's people."

Jack smiled. Annie's words made him feel better.

Arf, arf! Teddy barked, as if to say *Let's go!*

"Okay, okay," said Jack.

He picked up the Pennsylvania book and pointed at a picture of Frog Creek.

"I wish we could go home to our people," he said.

The wind started to blow.

The tree house started to spin.

It spun faster and faster.

Then everything was still.

Absolutely still.

10

Good Medicine

"We're home," said Annie.

Bright sunlight flooded the tree house. Teddy licked Jack's and Annie's faces. They were back in their jeans and T-shirts.

"Hey, silly," Annie said to the dog. "Now we have the second thing to help free you from your spell."

She took the eagle's feather out of Jack's backpack. She put it on Morgan's note, next to the silver pocket watch from the *Titanic*.

"Now we have our gift from the prairie blue," said Jack. "Let your thoughts rise as high as this feather."

"Hey, I just had a thought!" said Annie.

"What?" said Jack.

"I bet Teddy had something to do with White Buffalo Woman," she said.

"Why?" asked Jack.

"One second Teddy disappeared in the grass. Then White Buffalo Woman appeared," said Annie. "When White Buffalo Woman disappeared, Teddy appeared."

"Hmm . . ." said Jack. He stared at the little dog.

Teddy tilted his head and gave Jack a wise look.

"Well . . ." said Jack, "maybe Teddy has good medicine."

"*Now* you understand," said Annie, smiling.

"Ja-ack! An-nie!" A call came from the distance.

Jack and Annie looked out the window of the tree house.

Their mom and their grandmother were standing on their porch.

"Yay, Grandmother's here!" said Annie.

"We're coming!" they shouted together.

"Let's put Teddy in your backpack," said Annie. "So we can take him home with us this time."

"Okay," said Jack.

But when they turned around, the little dog was gone.

"Teddy?" said Annie.

There was no sign of him.

"Oh, man, as soon as we turned our backs,

he slipped away," said Jack. "Just like last time."

"Don't worry," said Annie. "He'll find us again soon. I'm sure of it." She started down the rope ladder.

Jack grabbed his pack and followed.

As they started for home, a wind gusted through the trees.

Jack stopped for a moment to look at the woods.

Branches waved their leaves.

Birds left the branches and swooped up into the blue sky.

Black Hawk's grandmother is right, he thought. *All things are related.*

"Jack!" called Annie.

"Coming!" said Jack.

He hurried to catch up with her.

Together they ran out of the Frog Creek
woods . . . up their street . . . and into their own
grandmother's arms.

THE LEGEND OF
WHITE BUFFALO WOMAN

Long ago, when the Lakota had no game to hunt, a beautiful woman in white buckskins appeared. She gave the chief of the tribe a special pipe. It had a buffalo carved on its round bowl and eagle feathers hanging from its long wooden stem.

White Buffalo Woman told the chief that the smoke from the sacred pipe would carry prayers to the Great Spirit. The Great Spirit would answer by helping the Lakota find buffalo to hunt.

White Buffalo Woman also said that the pipe smoke would join all living things to the Lakota tribe.

The pipe bowl represented the earth.

The buffalo carved upon it represented all four-legged animals that live upon the earth.

The pipe's wooden stem represented all that grows on the earth.

The twelve eagle feathers hanging from it represented all the winged creatures.

As White Buffalo Woman walked away from the tribe, she turned into a white buffalo calf— one of the rarest animals of all.

The legend of White Buffalo Woman has been handed down from generation to generation by Lakota people.

MORE FACTS FOR YOU AND JACK

1) The Lakota tribe has also been called the Sioux.

2) Today most Lakota live on reservations in North and South Dakota. ("Reservations" are areas of land reserved for Native Americans by the U.S. government.) Lakota parents and grandparents still pass on the traditional beliefs of their people to their children.

3) The true name of the buffalo is *bison*. Bison came to North America during the Ice Age and at one time were the biggest group of large mammals on the continent.

4) In the 1800s, the U.S. Army was at war with the Native Americans of the plains.

They knew the Native American way of life could not survive without the bison. So they decided to kill all the herds. In the years that followed, millions of bison were killed until there were only a few hundred left.

5) In the early 1900s, many people wcrc upset by the killing of the bison. They asked the government to help save these animals. Captive bison were sent to Yellowstone National Park and protected from hunters. Almost 2,500 bison live there today.

Here's a special preview of

Magic Tree House® #19

TIGERS AT TWILIGHT

Jack and Annie meet ferocious
tigers in the jungle of India!

1

How Far Away?

Jack and Annie walked past the Frog Creek woods on their way home from the library.

"I miss Teddy," said Annie.

"Me, too," said Jack.

"He's a really smart dog," said Annie.

"Yeah," said Jack, "and brave."

"And wise," said Annie.

"And funny," said Jack.

"And here!" said Annie.

"What?" said Jack.

"*Here!*" Annie pointed at the Frog Creek woods.

A small dog with tan-colored fur was peeking out from the bushes.

Arf! Arf! he barked.

"Oh, wow! Teddy!" said Jack.

The little dog ran off into the woods.

"Let's go!" said Annie.

She and Jack raced after Teddy. The Frog Creek woods glowed with late afternoon sunlight.

The dog ran between the trees and finally

stopped at a rope ladder. It hung from the tallest oak tree and led up to the magic tree house.

Teddy waited for Jack and Annie to catch up. He panted and wagged his tail.

"Hi, you!" cried Annie. She picked up the little dog and hugged him. "We missed you!"

"Yeah, silly!" said Jack. He kissed Teddy. Teddy licked his face.

"Is it time to get our *third* gift?" asked Annie.

Teddy sneezed, as if to say, *Of course!*

Annie grabbed the rope ladder and started up. Jack put Teddy inside his backpack and followed.

They climbed into the tree house. There was the note from Morgan le Fay. It was on the floor, just where it had been two days ago.

Jack let Teddy out of his pack.

Annie picked up the note and read:

This little dog is under a spell and needs your help. To free him, you must be given four special things:

A gift from a ship lost at sea,
A gift from the prairie blue,
A gift from a forest far away,
A gift from a kangaroo.

Be wise. Be brave. Be careful.

Morgan

Jack touched the first two gifts, which they had already gotten: a pocket watch from the *Titanic* and an eagle's feather from the Lakota Indians of the Great Plains.

"Now we have to get the gift from a forest far away," said Annie.

"I wonder *how* far away?" said Jack.

"I know how to find out," said Annie. "Where's our book?"

She and Jack looked around the tree house for one of the research books that Morgan always left them.

Arf! Arf! Teddy pawed a book in the corner.

Jack picked it up and read the title: *Wildlife of India.*

"Oh, man. India," he said. "That's *very* far away."

"Let's get going," said Annie, "so we can free Teddy."

Jack pointed at the cover of the book.

"I wish we could go there," he said.

The wind started to blow.

The tree house started to spin.

It spun faster and faster.
Then everything was still.
Absolutely still.
But only for a moment . . .

Magic Tree House®

Magic Tree House® Merlin Missions

Magic Tree House®
Super Edition

#1: WORLD AT WAR, 1944

Magic Tree House®
Fact Trackers

DINOSAURS
KNIGHTS AND CASTLES
MUMMIES AND PYRAMIDS
PIRATES
RAIN FORESTS
SPACE
TITANIC
TWISTERS AND OTHER TERRIBLE STORMS
DOLPHINS AND SHARKS
ANCIENT GREECE AND THE OLYMPICS
AMERICAN REVOLUTION
SABERTOOTHS AND THE ICE AGE
PILGRIMS
ANCIENT ROME AND POMPEII
TSUNAMIS AND OTHER NATURAL DISASTERS
POLAR BEARS AND THE ARCTIC
SEA MONSTERS
PENGUINS AND ANTARCTICA
LEONARDO DA VINCI
GHOSTS
LEPRECHAUNS AND IRISH FOLKLORE
RAGS AND RICHES: KIDS IN THE TIME OF
    CHARLES DICKENS
SNAKES AND OTHER REPTILES
DOG HEROES
ABRAHAM LINCOLN

PANDAS AND OTHER ENDANGERED SPECIES
HORSE HEROES
HEROES FOR ALL TIMES
SOCCER
NINJAS AND SAMURAI
CHINA: LAND OF THE EMPEROR'S GREAT
    WALL
SHARKS AND OTHER PREDATORS
VIKINGS
DOGSLEDDING AND EXTREME SPORTS
DRAGONS AND MYTHICAL CREATURES
WORLD WAR II

More Magic Tree House®

GAMES AND PUZZLES FROM THE TREE HOUSE
MAGIC TRICKS FROM THE TREE HOUSE
MY MAGIC TREE HOUSE JOURNAL
MAGIC TREE HOUSE SURVIVAL GUIDE
ANIMAL GAMES AND PUZZLES
MAGIC TREE HOUSE INCREDIBLE FACT BOOK

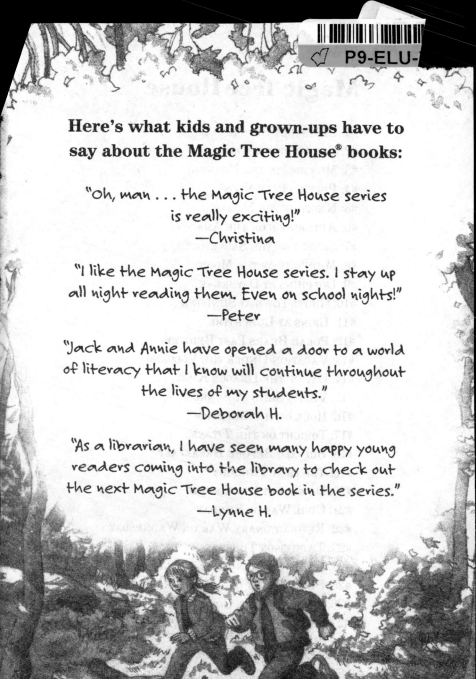

Here's what kids and grown-ups have to say about the Magic Tree House® books:

"Oh, man . . . the Magic Tree House series
is really exciting!"
—Christina

"I like the Magic Tree House series. I stay up
all night reading them. Even on school nights!"
—Peter

"Jack and Annie have opened a door to a world
of literacy that I know will continue throughout
the lives of my students."
—Deborah H.

"As a librarian, I have seen many happy young
readers coming into the library to check out
the next Magic Tree House book in the series."
—Lynne H.

Magic Tree House®

For a list of Magic Tree House® Merlin Missions and other Magic Tree House® titles, visit MagicTreeHouse.com.

MAGIC TREE HOUSE®

#28 HIGH TIDE IN HAWAII

BY MARY POPE OSBORNE
ILLUSTRATED BY SAL MURDOCCA

A STEPPING STONE BOOK™

Random House 🏠 New York

For Mel and Dana

Text copyright © 2003 by Mary Pope Osborne
Cover art and interior illustrations copyright © 2003 by Sal Murdocca

All rights reserved. Published in the United States by Random House Children's Books, a division of Penguin Random House LLC, New York.

Random House and the colophon are registered trademarks and A Stepping Stone Book and the colophon are trademarks of Penguin Random House LLC. Magic Tree House is a registered trademark of Mary Pope Osborne; used under license.

Visit us on the Web!
MagicTreeHouse.com
SteppingStonesBooks.com

Library of Congress Cataloging-in-Publication Data
Osborne, Mary Pope.
High tide in Hawaii / by Mary Pope Osborne ; illustrated by Sal Murdocca. — 1st ed.
p. cm. — (Magic tree house ; #28) A stepping stone book.
Summary: Jack and Annie travel in their magic tree house back to a Hawaiian island of long ago where they make friends, learn how to surf, and encounter a tsunami.
ISBN 978-0-375-80616-2 (trade) — ISBN 978-0-375-90616-9 (lib. bdg.) —
ISBN 978-0-375-89485-5 (ebook)
[1. Hawaii—History—Fiction. 2. Time travel—Fiction. 3. Magic—Fiction.
4. Brothers and sisters—Fiction. 5. Tree houses—Fiction.] I. Murdocca, Sal, ill.
II. Title. III. Series: Osborne, Mary Pope. Magic tree house series ; v #28.
PZ7.O81167 Hi 2003 [Fic]—dc21 2002013781

Printed in the United States of America
43 42 41 40 39

This book has been officially leveled by using the F&P Text Level Gradient™ Leveling System.

Random House Children's Books supports the First Amendment and celebrates the right to read.

Contents

Prologue

One summer day in Frog Creek, Pennsylvania, a mysterious tree house appeared in the woods.

Eight-year-old Jack and his seven-year-old sister, Annie, climbed into the tree house. They found that it was filled with books.

Jack and Annie soon discovered that the tree house was magic. It could take them to the places in the books. All they had to do was point to a picture and wish to go there. While they are gone, no time at all passes in Frog Creek.

Along the way, Jack and Annie discovered that the tree house belongs to Morgan le Fay. Morgan is a magical librarian of Camelot, the long-ago kingdom of King Arthur. She travels through time and space, gathering books.

Jack and Annie have many exciting adventures helping Morgan and exploring different times and places. In Magic Tree House Books #25–28, they learn the art of magic. . . .

1

A Ship?

Jack and Annie were sitting on their porch, reading books. Jack was reading about gorillas. Annie was reading about Pilgrims.

Suddenly Annie closed her book. She looked up into the sunset.

"Hey!" Annie said with a smile.

Jack looked over at her.

"It's back!" she said, jumping up.

"Oh, man," breathed Jack. He knew she was talking about the magic tree house.

3

Annie could always tell when it was back.

Jack closed his book and stood up.

"We're going to the woods!" he called through the screen door. "There's something we have to check on!"

"Be back before dark!" their mom said.

"We will!" said Jack.

He picked up his backpack. Then he and Annie headed across the yard. When they got to the sidewalk, they started running. They ran up their street and into the Frog Creek woods.

In the last light of day, they hurried between the trees. Finally, they came to the tallest oak. They held their breath as they looked up.

The magic tree house *was* back.

"Good going," said Jack.

"Thanks!" said Annie.

She started up the ladder. Jack followed. It was nearly dark inside. But the sun-dried wood smelled like a summer day.

"What kind of special magic will we look for this time?" said Jack.

They glanced around the tree house. They saw the scrolls they'd brought back from Shakespeare's theater. They saw the twig from the mountain gorillas and the pouch of corn seeds from the first Thanksgiving.

"There!" said Annie. She pointed to a book in the corner. A piece of paper was sticking out of it.

Jack picked up the book. Then he pulled out the paper and read:

Dear Jack and Annie,

Good luck on your fourth journey to find

*a special magic. This secret rhyme will
guide you:*

> *To find a special magic,*
> *build a special kind of ship*
> *that rides the waves,*
> *both high and low,*
> *on every kind of trip.*

> > *Thank you,*
> > *Morgan*

Jack looked at Annie.

"A ship?" he said.

She shrugged. "Yep. I guess we have to
build a ship. Where do we go to build it?"

She and Jack looked at the book's cover. It
showed palm trees, a beach, and a beautiful
ocean. The title was:

A VISIT TO OLD HAWAII

"Oh, wow!" said Annie. "I *love* Hawaii!"

"How do you know you love it?" Jack asked. "We've never been to Hawaii."

"Well, we're going now!" said Annie. She pointed at the cover. "We wish we could go there!"

The wind started to blow.

The tree house started to spin.

It spun faster and faster.

Then everything was still.

Absolutely still.

2

Aloha!

Jack opened his eyes. A gentle wind brushed against his skin. It smelled sweet and fresh.

Annie looked out the window. "Nice!" she said.

Jack looked out, too. The tree house had landed on top of a tall palm tree. The palm tree was at the edge of a flowery meadow.

On one side of the meadow, a cliff dropped down to the beach and ocean. On the other side of the meadow were the rooftops of a small village.

Beyond the village were tall gray mountains. Misty clouds hid their peaks. Waterfalls gushed down their sides.

"I *told* you I loved Hawaii!" said Annie. "Don't you?"

"I have to learn about it first," said Jack. He pushed his glasses into place and opened their research book. He read aloud:

> Hawaii is a chain of islands in the Pacific Ocean. The largest island is Hawaii, which gives its name to the whole group. The islands were formed millions of years ago by volcanoes. The volcanoes erupted under the

**ocean. Over time, their craters rose
above the water.**

"Wow," said Annie. "We're on the top of a volcano."

"Yeah," said Jack. He read on:

**The volcanic rock crumbled and
turned to soil. Over millions of years,
wind and birds dropped seeds on the
islands. Plants and trees began to
grow, and birds and insects made
their homes.**

"Cool," said Jack. He took out his notebook and pencil and wrote:

wind and birds brought seeds

He read some more:

About two thousand years ago, people

11

first came to Hawaii. They came in canoes from other islands in the Pacific. They rowed for thousands of miles across the ocean, guided only by the wind and stars.

"Hey, listen," said Annie.

Jack put down the book and listened. Sounds of music and laughter floated on the breeze.

"There must be a party in that village," said Annie. "Let's go."

"What about building that ship?" asked Jack.

"We'll figure that out later," said Annie. "Let's meet some people at the party. Maybe they can help us."

She started down the ladder.

Jack heard a whoop of laughter in the distance. *The party does sound fun,* he thought.

He packed up his things and followed Annie down to the ground.

The sun was low in the sky. They walked through the meadow toward the village. Everything was bathed in a golden red glow.

"Oh, man," breathed Jack.

There was beauty everywhere: purple flowers shaped like bells, white flowers that looked like stars, tall, feathery ferns, green spiky plants, big orange-and-black butterflies, and tiny yellow birds.

When they got close to the village, they saw an open area filled with people. Jack and Annie slipped behind a palm tree. They peeked out at the party.

There were about fifty people, including grown-ups, teenagers, and little kids. They were all barefoot and wore wreaths of flowers around their necks.

A woman was chanting. Her words rose and fell like waves. She chanted about a volcano goddess named Pele.

While she chanted, other people played music. Some blew on pipes that looked like flutes. Others shook gourds that sounded like baby rattles. Some hit sticks together to make clicking sounds.

Most of the villagers were dancing to the music. They stepped from side to side. They swayed their hips and waved their hands.

"They're doing the hula," whispered Annie. She smiled and waved her hands, too.

"Don't get carried away," whispered Jack.

He took out their book and found a picture of Hawaiians dancing. He read:

The early Hawaiians had no written language. They told stories with hula

dancing. The hula is a blend of dancing and chanting poetry.

Jack pulled out his notebook. He started a list about early Hawaii:

no written language

stories with hula

Suddenly Jack heard loud laughter and clapping. He looked up. Annie was gone!

Jack peeked out from behind the tree. Annie was doing the hula with the dancers! But no one seemed surprised. Everyone just smiled at her as they kept dancing.

A girl caught sight of Jack. She looked about Annie's age. She had long, shiny black hair and a big, friendly smile.

"Come do the hula!" she called to him.

"No way," Jack breathed.

He slipped behind the tree again. But the girl danced over to him and took his hand.

"Join us!" she said.

"No thanks," said Jack.

The girl didn't let go. She pulled Jack into the open. The music got louder. The dancers and musicians nodded and smiled at Jack.

Jack stood still. He didn't know how to do *any* kind of dance, let alone the hula! He stared at the ground, clutching his backpack and notebook until the music and dancing ended.

The Hawaiians gathered around Jack and Annie. They all had friendly, open faces.

"Who are you?" the young girl asked.

"I'm Annie," said Annie. "This is my brother, Jack."

"I'm Kama," the girl said. "This is my brother, Boka." She pointed to a boy in the crowd who looked about Jack's age.

The boy stepped forward. He grinned a big grin just like his sister's. He pulled off his wreath of red fluffy flowers. He put it around Annie's neck.

"A *lei* to welcome you," Boka said.

Kama then pulled off her lei and put it around Jack's neck.

"*Aloha*, Jack and Annie!" everyone said.

3
Sleepover

"*Aloha,*" said Jack and Annie.

"Where did you come from?" a pretty woman asked.

"Frog—" Annie started.

But Jack broke in. "From over the mountains," he said quickly. He pointed at the mountains looming in the distance.

"We are glad you have come to visit us," the woman said.

Everyone smiled and nodded.

They're all amazingly nice, Jack thought.

The music started again. As people began to dance, Kama took Annie's hand.

"Sit and talk with us," she said.

She and Boka led Jack and Annie to the edge of the clearing. They sat cross-legged in the grass. Kama picked up a wooden bowl. She held it out.

"Please eat," she said.

"What is it?" asked Annie.

"It is *poi*," said Kama. She scooped some poi out of the bowl and licked it off of her fingers.

"You eat it with your hands? Cool," said Annie. She stuck her fingers in the bowl and licked off the poi. "Mmm . . . good."

Jack stuck his finger in the bowl, too. The gooey mixture felt like peanut butter. But when he licked it off his finger, it had a weird taste—both bitter and sweet.

"Hmm," he said, but he made a face.

"He doesn't like it," Kama said to Boka.

"No, no," said Jack. "It's . . ." He tried to think of something polite. . . . "It's very interesting."

Kama and Boka giggled. Then they stuck their fingers in the bowl and ate some poi.

"Interesting!" they exclaimed. They cracked up laughing. Jack and Annie laughed with them.

"Now tell us about your home over the mountains," said Kama, "this place you call 'Frog.'"

Kama's friendly smile made Jack want to tell her the truth.

"It's actually called Frog Creek," he said. "It's very far away—much farther than just over the mountains. We traveled here in a magic tree house."

21

Kama's and Boka's eyes got huge. They smiled even bigger smiles than before.

"That sounds fun!" said Kama.

"You are so lucky!" said Boka.

Jack and Annie laughed.

"Yeah, we are," said Jack. He felt great telling their new friends about the tree house. He and Annie had never talked about it with their friends back home.

"Can you stay here tonight?" asked Kama.

Jack shrugged. "Sure, we can stay at least one night," he said.

Kama hurried over to the pretty woman. They spoke together for a moment. Then Kama returned to Jack and Annie.

"Our mother invites you to sleep at our house," she said.

"Great," said Annie. "Thanks."

Jack and Annie stood up. In the gray twilight, they followed Kama and Boka through the village. They wove between small huts with steep roofs until Kama stopped in front of one.

"This is our house," she said.

The hut had no door—just a wide entrance that opened into one large room.

Kama and Boka led Jack and Annie inside. In the dim light, Jack could barely see the dried-grass walls and the woven-grass mats on the dirt floor.

"Where do we sleep?" he asked.

"Here!" said Boka.

He and Kama lay down on the mats. Annie pulled off her lei and shoes. Then she lay down, too.

"Oh," said Jack. "Okay."

He took off his shoes and wreath of flowers. He used his backpack as a pillow when he lay down. The warm wind rustled the palm leaves outside. Music drifted in from the party.

"The ocean is calling," said Kama.

Jack could barely hear the waves in the distance.

"Tomorrow we will take you wave riding," said Boka.

"You mean *surfing*?" said Annie.

"Yes," said Kama.

"Cool," said Jack. But he wasn't sure he meant it. Surfing actually seemed pretty scary.

Kama seemed to hear his thoughts. "Don't worry," she said. "We'll have fun."

"No kidding," said Annie.

Soon Jack heard steady breathing. The other kids had fallen asleep.

Oh darn, we forgot to ask them about building a ship, he thought. *I guess we'll have to do that tomorrow. . . .*

Jack closed his eyes and yawned. Soon he, too, was fast asleep.

4

Garden Paradise

Jack heard pounding noises. He imagined Boka and Kama were building a ship.

He opened his eyes. Only he and Annie were still in the hut. A piece of cloth covered the doorway. Jack sat up and shook Annie.

"Wake up!" he said.

She opened her eyes.

"I think they're building a ship outside," said Jack. "Come on, let's go."

Annie jumped up.

26

"Don't forget your lei," she said.

They put on their flower wreaths. Jack lifted the cloth over the doorway, and they stepped out into the warm sunlight.

Boka, Kama, and their parents smiled at Jack and Annie. They were all working. But no one was building a ship.

Boka was pounding a wide strip of bark with a wooden club. Kama was using a stone to pound something that looked like a fat sweet potato. Their parents were weaving grass mats.

"What are you making?" Jack asked.

"I'm making *tapa*," said Boka. "First I beat the bark of the mulberry tree into thin sheets. Then my father pastes the sheets together to make cloth for us."

"This is the root of a *taro* plant," said

Kama. She pointed at the squashed white vegetable. "When you add fruit to it, you get poi."

"Great," said Jack. "By the way, do you ever build ships?"

"Ships?" asked Boka. "What for?"

Jack shrugged. "To sail away?" he said.

"Why would we do that?" asked Kama.

"Good question," said Jack, smiling.

"Can I help?" Annie asked Kama.

"Sure," said Kama. While she showed Annie how to pound the taro root, Jack slipped back into the hut. He pulled out his notebook and quickly added to his Hawaii list:

tapa—bark pounded into cloth

taro root—pounded for poi

ship—?

Jack heard Kama ask her parents if they could play now.

"We've finished our chores," said Kama. "May we take Jack and Annie to the ocean?"

"For wave riding," said Boka.

Jack held his breath. He half hoped their parents would say no.

"Yes, go have a good time with your friends," said their father.

"Come on, Jack!" Annie called.

Jack put his notebook away. He pulled on his pack and joined the others outside.

"We'll be back in a little while," said Kama.

"Don't forget to eat breakfast!" said her mother.

"We won't," said Kama.

Where will we get breakfast? wondered Jack.

He and Annie followed Kama and Boka. They passed villagers hard at work. Some carried firewood or water. Others were cutting grass or stripping bark from trees. Everyone smiled and waved.

"Hungry?" Kama asked Jack and Annie.

"Sure," they said.

Kama and Boka went into the grove of

palms near the huts. They climbed up two slanting tree trunks, using their hands and feet to push themselves up. At the top, they shook the palm leaves.

"Watch out!" Kama shouted.

Jack and Annie jumped back as big, round coconuts fell to the ground.

Kama and Boka slid down the trees. They each picked up a coconut. Then they found rocks and began to whack the hard shells. They whacked and whacked until their coconuts cracked into halves.

Kama shared hers with Annie. Boka shared his with Jack.

Jack drank the fresh, sweet milk inside the coconut. "Mmm!" he said.

"Interesting?" asked Boka.

"No. *Mmm* means *good!*" said Jack.

Everyone laughed.

Then Kama picked bananas off a banana tree and gave them to Jack and Annie. Jack peeled his and took a bite. It was the best banana he'd ever eaten.

When breakfast was over, they all headed into the flowery meadow. The sky was the bluest blue Jack had ever seen. The grass was the greenest green. The flowers and birds sparkled like jewels.

Hawaii is like a garden paradise, Jack thought.

He wanted to look up Hawaiian birds and flowers in the research book. As the others kept walking, he stopped and pulled out the book.

"Jack! Come look!" Annie shouted. She was standing at the edge of a cliff with Boka and Kama.

Jack put away the book and hurried to join

the others. He looked down at a beach fifty feet below.

There were no people. Only seashells and seaweed lay on the glistening white sand. Big, foamy waves crashed against the shore.

"Wow!" said Annie.

Uh-oh, thought Jack.

5
GO!

Boka looked at Jack and grinned.

"Ready?" he asked.

"I'm ready!" said Annie. "Where do we get our surfboards?"

"Down there," said Kama. She pointed to a rocky path that led to the beach.

"Let's go," said Annie.

Annie, Boka, and Kama started down the path. Jack followed, moving slowly and carefully.

When he stepped onto the beach, Jack slipped off his shoes. He dug his toes into the dry, warm sand. It felt as soft as silk.

"Actually, I wouldn't mind just taking a walk on the beach," he said to the others.

But no one seemed to hear. They had all walked over to a row of wooden surfboards propped against the rocks.

Boka picked out a long board and lugged it over to Jack. "For you," he said.

Jack took the board and looked up at it. It was as tall as his dad.

"Isn't this a little *big* for me?" he asked.

Boka shook his head. He chose a board for Annie. Then he and Kama grabbed a couple for themselves.

Jack took a deep breath. "I'd like to read a little about surfing first," he said. He put his board down and pulled out the research book.

"What is *that*?" asked Kama.

"It's a book," said Jack. "It tells you about things."

"How does it talk?" said Kama.

"It doesn't talk," said Annie. "You read it."

Kama looked confused.

"Jack, forget the book now," Annie said. "Let's just do what Boka and Kama tell us." She headed for the ocean, lugging her board.

Jack sighed and put the book away. He left his pack in the sand, picked up his board, and followed the others.

They all stopped at the edge of the water.

"First we need to get past the breaking

waves," said Kama. "Then we'll show you what to do next."

Together they waded into the cool, shallow water. *The waves don't seem all that big*, Jack thought hopefully.

But as he waded deeper into the ocean, the breaking waves began to look bigger and bigger. When the first wave hit him, Jack leaned against it, lifting his board. He nearly fell over.

Kama, Boka, and Annie moved farther out into the ocean. Jack watched as a wave loomed over them. They all threw their boards over the wave and dove into it.

Jack struggled forward. The next time a big wave came toward him, he threw his board over it. Holding his glasses tightly, he ducked under.

When Jack stood up again, he wiped the water from his eyes and glasses. His surfboard was close by. He grabbed it before another wave came.

Jack kept fighting his way forward. By the time he got past all the breakers, the water was up to his chest.

"We'll paddle out to catch a big wave!" said Boka.

Jack frowned. "But—"

"Don't worry, Jack," said Kama. "It will be fun!"

Boka and Kama pulled themselves onto their boards. They lay on their bellies and began paddling with their hands out to sea.

Jack and Annie lay down on their boards, too. Paddling over the gentle waves, Jack relaxed. Now, *this* was something he could do all day.

"When I say *go*, paddle fast back toward the shore!" said Kama.

"When do we stand up?" said Annie.

"When you start toward the shore!" said Boka. "Stand up with one foot forward. Stretch out your arms to keep your balance!"

"But don't try to stand up the very first time!" said Kama. "Just ride your board on your belly!"

"I see one coming now!" said Boka.

"Wait, wait!" said Jack. Everything was happening too fast. He had questions.

"*Go!*" Kama shouted.

Jack saw a big wave rolling toward them. Before he knew it, Boka, Kama, and Annie were paddling quickly toward the shore. Jack paddled like crazy to keep up.

Suddenly the wave lifted him and swept him forward! Jack zoomed toward the shore with amazing speed. Out of the corner of his eye, he saw Boka and Kama—*and* Annie!— all standing up.

Jack wanted to be like them. In a flash, he went up on his knees. He put his left foot forward and stood up! For one second he felt like a soaring bird—then he lost his balance!

Jack fell into the water, grabbing his glasses just in time. The wave crashed down on top of him! Water filled his mouth and went up his nose. His board and his lei were swept away.

Jack twisted and turned in the churning water. When his head bobbed up above the water, he choked and coughed.

Another big wave crashed down on him, and he went under again. When he came up, he plunged forward, desperately trying to get to shore.

Again and again, Jack was thrown down and slammed by breaking waves. But each time, he got up and hurled himself closer to shore.

Finally, Jack dragged himself out of the ocean. Feeling bruised and battered, he fell onto the sand.

6

Shake-up

"Jack!" cried Annie. She ran to him. "Are you okay?"

Jack just nodded. He put on his wet glasses. He felt shaky and mad at himself. *never should have tried to stand!* he thought.

Kama picked up Jack's surfboard from the shallow water and brought it over to him.

"I told you not to stand," she said, laughing. "You fell hard."

It's not funny, thought Jack. *I nearly drowned!*

"The best thing to do is to go right back out," said Boka.

"You go," said Jack. His eyes and nose burned from the salt water. "I'll stay here." He walked over to his pack, picked it up, and took out the research book.

"Come on, Jack!" said Annie. "Try it again! Stay on your belly this time!"

"No, this time I'm going to *read* about surfing first," he said.

"Aw, you should just try it again," said Annie. "Not *read* about it!"

She ran to him and pulled the book out of his hands. Jack jerked it away from her. He slipped and fell onto the sand.

Kama and Boka laughed again.

"Why are you laughing?" Jack snapped. 'You don't even know how to read!"

Boka and Kama looked hurt.

"Jack!" said Annie. "That was mean. Say you're sorry."

Jack opened his book and pretended to read it. He *did* feel sorry, but he was too upset to say so.

"Fine, stay here," said Annie. She went back to Boka and Kama. "Let's go."

As Jack sat alone on the beach, he looked up from his book. He watched the other kids paddling through the water.

"I don't care," he muttered. "I'm *never* going back out in those waves."

Morgan didn't send us here to surf any-way, he thought. *She told us to build a ship. But how the heck are we supposed to do that?*

Jack heaved an angry sigh. Now he was cross with Morgan. He turned to the back of the book and searched the index for "ship."

Suddenly Jack heard a rumbling from under the sand. The ground started to shake. It shook so hard, the book flew out of Jack's hands!

Jack bounced up and down on the beach. Shells were jumping up and down, too. Rocks tumbled down from the cliff.

It's an earthquake! thought Jack.

The rumbling stopped.

The shaking stopped.

Jack looked around. Everything was normal again, except some rocks rolled around at the bottom of the cliff.

Jack looked out to sea. Kama, Boka, and Annie were past the breakers. They were sitting on their surfboards, laughing and talking.

Everything seemed okay. But Jack felt

sure that something was wrong. He grabbed the Hawaii book from the sand. He looked up "earthquake." He read:

> Earthquakes in Hawaii have been known to cause tsunamis (soo-NAH-meez), which used to be called "tidal waves." An earthquake can cause water out at sea to be set in motion. The water grows higher and higher as it moves toward land. Just before the tsunami strikes, water may pull away from the shore. Then it returns in a gigantic wave that crashes over the land and washes everything away.

Oh, man! thought Jack. *A tsunami might be coming!*

7

Ride for Your Lives!

Jack had to find out more about tsunamis quickly. He read as fast as he could:

A tsunami can strike a few hours—or a few minutes!—after an earthquake. It depends on the strength of the earthquake and where it took place. After earthquakes, it is safest for islanders to seek higher ground.

We have to get to higher ground now! thought Jack, dropping the book.

He ran down to the edge of the ocean. Boka, Kama, and Annie were still paddling out beyond the waves. Jack forgot all about their fight.

"Hey, you guys!" he yelled.

They didn't hear him.

Jack went into the shallow water. "Hey, you guys!" he yelled. "Come back!"

They still didn't hear him.

Jack ran to his surfboard, grabbed it, and ran into the ocean. He fought the breaking waves. Once he was past them, he threw himself on his board and paddled wildly.

The wave swells grew as he paddled. He could hardly see Annie, Boka, or Kama over them. Jack paddled faster and faster, trying to reach them.

"Hey!" he yelled. *"Hey!"*

Boka looked back at him. He gave Jack a friendly wave, then turned away again.

I have to get them to come to me! Jack thought frantically. "HELP! HELP!" he yelled at the top of his lungs.

The three kids jerked around. They paddled quickly toward Jack with worried faces.

"What's wrong?" Annie cried when they got closer. "Are you in trouble?"

"We *all* are!" said Jack. "A tsunami might be coming! There was an earthquake when I was on the beach!"

"We'd better ride in fast!" said Boka.

"Stay on your bellies!" said Kama. "It's safer!"

"Here comes a wave!" cried Boka.

They all started paddling.

The swell of the wave picked them up.

They were all swept forward!

Jack gripped the sides of his board as he zoomed along with the others. Suddenly he dropped down as the wave curled under. It felt like a roller coaster! But he stayed on his board as the wave carried him to shore.

Jack rolled off into the shallow water. He snatched up his board and ran onto the sand. Boka and Kama were waiting.

"Good riding, Jack!" said Boka.

"Where's Annie?" asked Jack.

Boka pointed. Annie was in the shallow water, pulling her board in. As they watched, something very weird began to happen to the ocean.

The water around Annie started to pull away.

8

The Big Wave

"Run, Annie!" Jack screamed.

The water drew away from the beach, and a loud hissing sound came from the sea.

Suddenly fish flopped on the bare sand!

Annie threw down her board and ran. She grabbed Jack's hand as she ran by him. Jack grabbed Boka's hand, and Boka grabbed Kama's hand. They all ran together, pulling each other along as they raced to the cliff.

Boka and Kama ran up the cliff path. Jack

and Annie grabbed their shoes and Jack's pack. Then they scrambled up the path, too.

At the top of the cliff, everyone looked back. Jack couldn't believe his eyes!

A wave was rising up like a dark mountain of water. It came surging toward the shore, growing even taller!

"*Wow*," whispered Annie.

"Get back!" shouted Boka.

The four of them bolted back from the edge of the rocky slope. The mountain of water crashed against the cliff. Water sprayed over the top of the rocks and rained down on them.

When the water rolled back over the cliff, they all hurried back to the edge to see what had happened.

The rocky cliff path was gone. The gigantic wave was moving back out to sea, taking rocks, sand, seaweed, seashells, and the surfboards with it.

"Scary," breathed Annie.

"Yeah," said Jack. "We just made it."

"Boka! Kama!" voices yelled.

They turned around. Jack saw Boka and

Kama's parents racing across the meadow toward them. Other villagers followed.

The two Hawaiian kids ran into their parents' arms. Soon Jack and Annie were surrounded by villagers. Everyone was laughing and crying and hugging each other.

Jack hugged Annie. He hugged Kama and Boka and their parents—and lots of other people he didn't even know.

9

Telling the Story

Finally, the hugging and crying and laughing died down. The villagers started walking back to their huts.

Jack and Annie followed Boka, Kama, and their parents.

"We felt the ground shaking," said Boka and Kama's father. "We knew a big wave might follow!"

"Jack saved us!" said Boka. "He read in a book and found out about the big waves."

"What's a book?" asked his mother.

"Show them," Annie said to Jack.

Jack reached into his pack and took out their research book.

"It tells about the big waves in here," he said. "Books give lots of information."

"Ah," said Boka and Kama's mother. "A book is a good thing."

"Books tell stories, too," said Annie.

"That is impossible," said Kama. "The book cannot move its feet or wave its hands. It cannot sing or chant."

"That's true," said Jack, smiling.

"Now we should do the hula," Boka said to Annie, Kama, and Jack, "and tell our story."

"I'll watch," said Jack, stepping away.

Boka and Kama's father called for music.

The villagers gathered around. A man

started to play a pipe. A teenage boy knocked two sticks together. Some women began shaking rattles.

Boka, Kama, and Annie waved their hands in time to the music. They stepped from side to side. They swayed their hips.

Kama chanted about going out into the water. She, Boka, and Annie waved their hands to show how they paddled out to sea.

Kama chanted about how Jack had warned them. She and the others waved their hands to show how they rode their surfboards to shore.

Then Jack surprised himself. He waved his hands to show how he rode his surfboard like a bird soaring through the air. The next thing he knew, he was stepping from side to side. He was swaying his hips. He was doing the hula!

Kama chanted about how the water had pulled away from the shore—and how they had climbed to safety—and how the giant wave had crashed against the cliff.

As Kama chanted the story, all the villagers joined in the dance. The tall grasses swayed. The palm trees swayed. And all the hula dancers swayed, too.

When the story ended, everyone clapped.

"Thanks for helping us," Boka said to Jack and Annie.

"We're a good team," said Annie.

"We are best friends," said Kama.

"Yeah," said Jack. "I'm sorry I said mean things."

"We're sorry we laughed at you," said Boka.

"I'm sorry I grabbed the book," said Annie.

"Our mother says friendship is like riding the waves," said Kama. "Sometimes you ride low, gentle waves. Sometimes you ride high, rough ones."

Annie gasped. She looked at Jack. She repeated Morgan's rhyme:

To find a special magic,
build a special kind of ship
that rides the waves,
both high and low,
on every kind of trip.

"*Friend*ship! That's the ship!" said Jack.

"And we built it!" said Annie.

She and Jack burst out laughing.

Boka and Kama looked a little confused, but they laughed, too.

"We have to go back to our own home now," Annie said to Boka and Kama.

"It's time to say good-bye," said Jack.

"We never say good-bye," said Kama. "We say aloha when we greet our friends. And we say aloha when we leave them."

"Friends are always together," said Boka,

"even when they are far apart."

"Have a good journey in your magic tree house," said Kama.

"Thanks," said Jack and Annie. They waved to all the villagers. *"Aloha!"*

"Aloha!" everyone called back.

Then Annie and Jack started through the meadow. Tiny yellow birds and orange-and-black butterflies flitted about them.

At the edge of the meadow, they came to the grove of palm trees. They climbed up the rope ladder into the tree house.

Out the window, Jack saw the tall mountains, the small village, the flowery meadow, and the ocean. The water was peaceful again.

"I still have my lei," said Annie.

She took it off. Though the red flowers were wet, they were still a little fluffy.

"It's proof that we found the special magic," said Jack. "The magic of friendship."

Annie put the lei on the floor next to the play scrolls, the twig, and the corn seeds. Then she picked up the Pennsylvania book.

"Ready?" she asked.

Jack sighed. "I love Hawaii," he said.

"*Finally*, you admit it," said Annie. She pointed at a picture of the Frog Creek woods. "I wish we could go home now."

The wind started to blow.

The tree house started to spin.

It spun faster and faster.

Then everything was still.

Absolutely still.

10

Everyday Magic

Jack opened his eyes.

The sun was setting beyond the woods. No time at all had passed in Frog Creek.

"Welcome back," said a soft, lovely voice.

Morgan le Fay was in the magic tree house.

"Morgan!" cried Annie. She threw her arms around the enchantress.

Jack hugged Morgan, too.

"Look, Morgan," said Annie. "We have proof we found four special kinds of magic!"

"Yes, I see," said Morgan.

Morgan picked up the play scrolls that Shakespeare had given Jack and Annie in old England.

"You found the *magic of theater*," she said.

Morgan picked up the twig from a mountain gorilla in the African cloud forest.

"And the *magic of animals*," she said.

Morgan picked up the pouch of corn seeds from their trip to the first Thanksgiving.

"And the *magic of community*," she said.

Finally, Morgan picked up the wreath of flowers from Kama and Boka.

"And you discovered the *magic of friendship*," she said.

Morgan looked at Jack and Annie for a long moment. "Listen carefully to what I'm about to tell you," she said.

"Yes?" They both leaned forward.

"You are now Magicians of Everyday Magic," said Morgan. "You have learned to find the magic in things you encounter on earth every day. There are many other forms of everyday magic. You never have to look far to find it. You only have to live your life to the fullest."

Jack and Annie nodded.

Soon you will be called upon to use your knowledge of Everyday Magic in the realm of fantasy."

"The realm of fantasy?" said Jack.

"Are we going back to Camelot?" said Annie.

Before Morgan could answer, a shout came from the distance. "Jack! Annie!"

"Our dad's calling," said Annie.

"You must go home now," said Morgan gently. "Rest—and get ready to test your powers. Your most exciting challenges are yet to come."

"Good-bye, Morgan," said Annie and Jack.

They hugged the enchantress. Then Jack took the Hawaii book out of his pack and gave it to Morgan. He put on his backpack and followed Annie down the ladder.

When they stepped onto the ground, there was a great roar above them. Jack and Annie looked up. A swirl of sparkling light lit the top of the tree.

Then the light was gone. The tree house was gone. Morgan le Fay was gone, too.

Jack and Annie didn't speak for a long moment. Then Jack broke the silence.

"Our most exciting challenges are yet to

come?" he said. "What do you think Morgan meant by that?"

"I don't know," said Annie.

"It sounds a little scary," said Jack

"That's okay. We can handle it," said Annie. She smiled. "We're *Magicians of Everyday Magic.*"

Jack smiled. "Yeah," he said. "I guess we are."

They walked out of the woods as the sun was setting. Down the street their mom and dad were standing on their front porch. They waved at Jack and Annie.

Jack felt a surge of happiness. *There's another kind of everyday magic,* he thought, *the magic of family.*

In that moment, it seemed the best magic of all.

HAWAII
TIMETABLE

Millions of years ago, volcanoes rose from the Pacific Ocean to form the islands of Hawaii.

Around 1,500 years ago, Polynesians came to Hawaii. They were the first people to discover the islands. They traveled over 3,000 miles in wooden canoes from other islands in the Pacific.

In 1778, an Englishman named Captain James Cook made the first recorded European visit to Hawaii.

On August 21, 1959, Hawaii became the fiftieth state of the United States.

Today, over 6 million tourists from all over the world visit Hawaii every year.

MORE FACTS FOR
JACK AND ANNIE AND *YOU*!

Tsunamis were once called "tidal waves." Scientists no longer call them that because the waves have nothing to do with tides.

The Pacific Tsunami Warning System alerts the public of earthquakes or other disturbances that take place at sea. It puts out warnings on radio and TV. Sirens may also sound warnings. The warnings alert people to stay away from beaches and move to higher ground.

When the first Polynesians arrived in the Hawaiian islands 1,500 years ago, they brought the custom of riding surfboards with them.

According to one ancient Hawaiian legend, hula dancing began when Pele, the goddess of volcanoes, told her younger sister, Laka, to dance. Laka is now known as the goddess of song and dance and as the patroness of hula dancers. Today, the hula is studied and practiced by people from many different cultures.

Because of Hawaii's isolation, many of its plants and birds and insects are found nowhere else on earth. Sadly, many of them today are on the U.S. endangered species list.

Here's a special preview of
Magic Tree House® Fact Tracker

Tsunamis
and Other Natural
Disasters

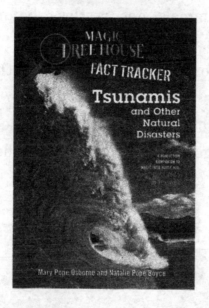

Help Jack and Annie track down facts
about natural disasters!

Available now!

Excerpt copyright © 2007 by Mary Pope Osborne and Natalie Pope Boyce. Illustrations
copyright © 2007 by Sal Murdocca. Published by Random House Children's Books,
a division of Penguin Random House LLC, New York.

Animal Warnings

For hundreds of years, people have noticed that animals get restless before earthquakes.

Before the 2004 tsunami hit, there were reports that dogs refused to go out. Bats flew around nervously during the day. And flamingos and other seabirds flew up to higher ground.

On the coast of Sumatra, elephant trainers claim their elephants began to cry. Then the elephants broke their chains and headed for the hills.

Scientists wonder if someday we can find a way for animals to actually help predict earthquakes. And if they can predict earthquakes, they can also warn us about tsunamis.

4
Volcanoes

The word *volcano* comes from Vulcan, the Roman god of fire. When we think of volcanoes, we often think of cone-shaped mountains spewing out fire and ash. But volcanoes come in different sizes and shapes. Some are tall mountains. Others are cracks in the earth. Still others are gentle slopes with a crater on top. Volcanoes are a vent, or opening in the earth's crust. Hot melted rock erupts from the vent.

Volcanoes form near the edges of plates. When subduction occurs, the lower plate can be pushed into the mantle. The temperature rises. New magma begins to form.

Magma is lighter than solid rock. It begins to rise up into the crust. Magma rises through passages called *conduits* (KAHN-doo-itz). The pressure from the rising magma builds up. It forces the magma, bits of rock, gas, and ash through the crust. When they reach the surface, the volcano suddenly erupts. Magma escapes from the

Ash cloud

Crater

Lava

Conduit

Vent

Magma chamber

opening of the volcano. When the magma hits open air, it is called *lava*.

Types of Eruptions

Not all volcanoes explode violently. The type of eruption depends on the lava itself. There are two kinds of lava. One type is thin and runny. Thin lava does not cause violent eruptions. It oozes slowly from the vent.

The second kind of lava is thick and sticky. It plugs up the volcano. Gases and steam are trapped under the magma. A huge amount of pressure builds as the gases and steam try to escape.

The gases behave like a bottle of soda when you shake it. Pressure builds up. When you open the soda, the pressure is released. And you'd better watch out or you'll get soaked!

What looks like smoke is actually ash shooting into the air.

Enough cool facts
to fill a tree house!

Jack and Annie have been all over the world in their adventures in the magic tree house. And they've learned lots of incredible facts along the way. Now they want to share them with you! Get ready for a collection of the weirdest, grossest, funniest, most all-around amazing facts that Jack and Annie have ever encountered. It's the ultimate fact attack!

Don't miss

Magic Tree House®
MERLIN MISSIONS #1

CHRISTMAS IN CAMELOT

Jack and Annie have to find the Water
of Memory and Imagination, which will
save Camelot from disappearing!

Magic Tree House®

#1: Dinosaurs Before Dark
#2: The Knight at Dawn
#3: Mummies in the Morning
#4: Pirates Past Noon
#5: Night of the Ninjas
#6: Afternoon on the Amazon
#7: Sunset of the Sabertooth
#8: Midnight on the Moon
#9: Dolphins at Daybreak
#10: Ghost Town at Sundown
#11: Lions at Lunchtime
#12: Polar Bears Past Bedtime
#13: Vacation Under the Volcano
#14: Day of the Dragon King
#15: Viking Ships at Sunrise
#16: Hour of the Olympics
#17: Tonight on the *Titanic*
#18: Buffalo Before Breakfast
#19: Tigers at Twilight
#20: Dingoes at Dinnertime
#21: Civil War on Sunday
#22: Revolutionary War on Wednesday
#23: Twister on Tuesday
#24: Earthquake in the Early Morning
#25: Stage Fright on a Summer Night
#26: Good Morning, Gorillas
#27: Thanksgiving on Thursday
#28: High Tide in Hawaii

Magic Tree House® Merlin Missions

#1: Christmas in Camelot
#2: Haunted Castle on Hallows Eve
#3: Summer of the Sea Serpent
#4: Winter of the Ice Wizard
#5: Carnival at Candlelight
#6: Season of the Sandstorms
#7: Night of the New Magicians
#8: Blizzard of the Blue Moon
#9: Dragon of the Red Dawn
#10: Monday with a Mad Genius
#11: Dark Day in the Deep Sea
#12: Eve of the Emperor Penguin
#13: Moonlight on the Magic Flute
#14: A Good Night for Ghosts
#15: Leprechaun in Late Winter
#16: A Ghost Tale for Christmas Time
#17: A Crazy Day with Cobras
#18: Dogs in the Dead of Night
#19: Abe Lincoln at Last!
#20: A Perfect Time for Pandas
#21: Stallion by Starlight
#22: Hurry Up, Houdini!
#23: High Time for Heroes
#24: Soccer on Sunday
#25: Shadow of the Shark
#26: Balto of the Blue Dawn
#27: Night of the Ninth Dragon

Magic Tree House®
Super Edition

Magic Tree House®
Fact Trackers

More Magic Tree House®